The Ladies

Sara Veglahn
The Ladies
A novel

NOEMI PRESS
LAS CRUCES, NEW MEXICO

Published By Noemi Press, Inc. A Nonprofit Literary Organization.
www.noemipress.org

Cover Design by Jana Vuković
Book Design by Steve Halle

First Edition
ISBN: 978-1-934819-70-8

For my grandmothers

Table of Contents

Invocation

Accidental Death, Breton Death Omens, Magpies, The Afterlife, Death of the Self, Death of the Dead Self, Reincarnation, Immortality, Resurrection, Tame Death, The Future of Death, Reconstructions of Death, Models of Death, Corpses Exposed in Tree Branches, Isles of the Dead, Smearing the Body with the Fat of the Dead, Bathing Ceremonies, Cremation, Mules, Being Buried Alive, Social Death, Private Death, Crows, Cultivating the Natural, Denial of Death, Disappearance, Dismemberment, Howling Dogs, Mummification, Laments, Passage, Purgatory, Exhumation, Reburial, Sacrificial Death, The Political Lives of Dead Bodies, Rope as Indication of the Deceased Soul, Sitting Shiva, Invisible Death, Negated Death, The Death Clock, Slipping Away, Near Death, Thanatos, Moths, Cats, Owls, Suttee, Sky Burial, Janazah, Kaddish, Laying to Rest, Funerary Pyre, Funerary Pyramid, Rosemary and Cinnabar, Marigolds and Lilies, Cutting the Abdomen and Taking Out the Heart, Forty-Nine Days, Fifty-One Days, One Hundred Days, Two Hundred and Sixty-Five Days, Yahrzeit, Collection of the Dead, A Large Black Coach Pulled by Four Black Horses, Banshees, Ankou, Coffin Ships, The Underworld

It Is Begun

The struggle of dying becomes the struggle of getting home.

To weep for someone still alive is a bad omen.

To whom it may concern: even though the end comes for everyone, even though no one lives forever, even though the final stage seems inevitable, everyone wants to deny it, wants to push away this thought, to smother it, to kill it. But not us. We seek it, desire it, wish upon a falling star, hope hope hope against hope.

In terms of forever, we are the rulers of the roost.

There is no way for us to be like other people.

Our task was given.

And the window frame rattles from the passing train our lives have become, a train crossing towns and counties and rivers and we watch from the window how the wilderness blurs, how the deep green blackens and grays, how roads and figures are rapid and swift in their standstill.

There were times we thought we could become something else, when we forgot our given task, when we forgot ourselves. In these moments, which were brief and infrequent, we were mirthful, we were birdlike, we squawked as we ran around our rooms cluttered with fabric and bells, but then the shift would happen, the wall would give way, for example, and we were confronted with the dark and the nearness of daybreak, the work of the earth roiling around on its axis, moving towards frost, towards heat, the seasons offering their deception, giving the impression that with a change in weather there would be a change in us too. And it was comforting to think so for a while. But then the river would churn forth ice and just as quickly fall prey to insects and overrunning its banks. When the river runs high, any amount of rain is dangerous. When the river begins, you cannot stop it.

The drums beat in time to the walkers who fill the streets and we walk too. We propel ourselves forward within the funerary rush. We hold our hats to our heads and bow down to the wind coming through hard and hot.

We must go. Again. Out into the world. Again, to the dark rooms where they lie. We go to them.

We were unable to stop. We couldn't avoid it. We were unable to stop in time. We were warned. Everyone seemed to know what was going to happen. Oh, you shouldn't go out there. Oh, it's terrible out there. Oh, you'd better be careful. Oh, you're gonna end up getting dragged out of a ditch. You're gonna fly off that bridge. You're gonna end up at the bottom of the river. Don't call me when you're stuck. Don't you dare call me. I'll just tell you I told you so.

But we stepped on the gas. We were all over. We stepped on the brakes. Gas and the swerve into everything they told us. And being unable. Everything that happened was invisible. Everything that happened was already.

Our car a truck   our car the other car   our car covered   our car in the middle   turned around   our car backed into   skidded over   too fast the bridge   and then the windshield   a warning   an approach without intention   we were learning to stop the road   the sudden appearance of the wrong way   power of the weather   power where no one should go without warning headed wheel to wheel   no one ever appeared that way   tumbling over the embankment   thought we were out the windows   thought we had been the windows   the thing we found ourselves in   what we saw was a different direction   what we saw was a corner   a signal   it couldn't be missed and we missed it   we were thrown   we ran so fast   we knew we were running so fast   but it felt slow   out of the road   into the wet   into the wrong house   we were wrong moving   sad in the ditch   in the water   and facing the way to say it: a stray tree it moved into our path like it had legs   we were off the hood all day   we wondered when we bobbed in the same place for weeks for months   we were waiting   we waited years for someone to come   we waited our whole lives   we were down there   we saw everything happen except for how to get up   and falling several times we reached our hands   our sleep intersected with wheels   and it was always dark there   no one to blame   we were told   we were thinking how we would explain   but we were like canaries and our little car our gilded cage we would never have got loose from   we flew differently when trouble began   we were caused to move too quickly   we told everyone we knew no injuries   fine everything fine   but we knew better   beneath our hats our skulls were slipping

Then it was dark.

We lay ourselves down on the riverbank and become damp in the mist off the water.

It is troublesome to find the beginning.

At first light, we head back to the house with its window glass gleaming, with its open door. Our humid trail evaporates in the heat of the day and we sit heavy around the table. Daylight fades. The clock ticks.

We walk, and our movement isn't like falling, it's like hunger. The trail an arrow pointing toward what we long to be. The trees with traces of wet on their dark trunks. The point from where we look, ancient, toward a return, together and taken, and mud covers our path. We long to be air, we are green still, understood as emitting green, bright in the morning, like a shot of fire across the sky. It's toward the grave, everything we imagine, what we think of as solid or what we think of as real. We were living, but now it's not possible. The morning far away from what we've realized. This was hours ago, the world of lingering, of overflowing. Look and see how we stand beside the car. And then the windows making everything pinkish and the sun failing, we are trying to be pointed toward something solid. The trees upward. The point before land. We walked gravely and then lost track of what we were supposed to understand. What in the hell were you doing there? We were sinking. We felt made up. An invention. We longed to be gathered, to be kept close, we are trying to keep close. Keep close now, don't you dare run off. You're sure to fall and I'm not coming down there to pull you out.

We would remain saints and sinners, priests and thieves. We smiled benevolently wearing green dresses, our hands clasped together over our breasts. We were zealous in our performance, fervent in our delivery. We were paid. These events took place behind heavy draperies, or in back rooms, or deep in cellars, or out of doors, or in a bright parlor, or just right there, in the living room, next to the television. Our virtue was never questioned. Everyone thought we were keys to heaven. They came from remote places or across town or across the street or around the corner to touch the hems of our garments, once we were finished and sent the departed on their way.

Our path was determined, it seems. Our tasks are unmistakable, we know. There isn't anything else. We are unsure why. We are caught.

We carry the bones and ashes. We eat the food placed before us. We eat and lick the plates clean. We are jealous of everyone. Understanding is far away and we cannot break free from how tired we are, how completely exhausted everything makes us. If we could rise with the sun in our faces and embrace the day, we might be able to think differently, we might be able to move through the world differently, we might be able to come to a conclusion, a resolution, a way out of this chamber in which we are kept.

We were scared to death, dead tired, dead cold, dead broke, a dead duck. We were red shifted. We donned a wooden overcoat. We were drop-dead gorgeous and dying to meet you. We nearly died, we were to die for. It was do or die, and we chucked the last nickel at the bridge. We were working the graveyard shift, we were turning over in our graves, it was quiet as a tomb, we were white as ghosts, and like shocks of corn fully ripened, we came to our coronations, and we were afraid we would never die.

We worried most about it at the age of ten, but at age seventeen, after it happened, we read about immortality and the feeling returned. It was unbearable. We simply could not bear it. Better to have total annihilation, anything, than this continual going on and on.

In the Country of the Living

We're here beneath rocks. The heaviest stones are on our chests. It is still unclear what should have happened when the shades were pulled, when the lights went out, when the kettle boiled, when the crocus bloomed, when we walked out the door, when we were waiting, when we were left waiting, when we were gone, down to the cellar, when the storm hit it was terrific, a bright star, our eyes took the blast, when we were young we wore flowers in our hair, it was always the same at the end of the season.

And our emergence was silent. We rose as high as the attic windows. As if we were on stilts, as if we didn't live in America, as if we didn't come from the river, as if we weren't already under water. We spent months thinking about isolation, invisibility, apparitions, different ways of speaking. We tried to understand everything before it happened, but we could never have prepared for what happened.

Until it erupted in us, we were what? New? Young? Ready and willing? This is only partly true. We were never willing. Our readiness was supplied by the intensive training we received, and yes, we were young, children really, and didn't know any better. We didn't know what it meant to do what we had been slated to do.

And how could we? There were no others like us, as far as we knew, except our teacher, and she was soon gone. Almost immediately upon completing our rigorous and singular education, hers was our first assignment. We couldn't know if we had done everything correctly. We couldn't be sure it had worked.

We were as if newly bloomed, as if in a garden of becoming. It was ridiculous. So bright and new. So clearly fated to stay.

At first we tried. At first we were eager to please, to master, to make sure. At first we gave all our efforts because even if we were proceeding wrongly, we could take comfort in having done our best.

But our best was only measured by ourselves. It became clear our expertise could be faked because it was unquestioned. They would believe anything, the ones we went to. They were so distraught, they often didn't acknowledge our departure and frequently didn't notice our arrival. We were merely a part of the shadows, the doors by which the dead pass through.

However, we didn't know this for a long time. It took us years to understand. Once we did, that's when it took hold. We could never return to our old way of thinking. We were stuck.

However, we appeared as if we were just like everyone else. It was impossible to discern any difference. We kept up with the latest fashions, had our hair cut in the styles shown in magazines, filled our speech with the current frivolous phrases and ridiculous intonations, and never once did we slip up or make a mistake or reveal that we were anything other than what was seen everywhere.

Our days were spent in the cafes, where we pretended to write in journals with sparkly covers and read romance novels, where we drank the fancy coffees other people drank, where we giggled and smirked and made faces at ourselves in the windows. Anyone observing us would think we were just another group of mindless, airy girls. Anyone overhearing our conversations would never know we were strangled by the dilemma of our situation. We looked carefree and coy. We acted stupid and superficial. We aspired to be a part of the club of girls who wanted to be noticed for their appearance and capacity for having fun—the girls who offered nothing more than witty remarks and provocative demeanors.

At home, we practiced. We were excellent mimics and had piles of notes we took surreptitiously out in the world, which we studied with the reverence of monks. This world was not ours, and so to understand, to merge into it, we made recordings and took photographs in grocery stores and restaurants and pet shops and nightclubs and bars and shopping malls and colleges and high schools and pedestrian bridges and pharmacies and freeways and beaches and airports and movie-theatre lines and public pools and pizza parlors and car washes and video arcades and on the subway and on the bus.

The way to falter. We caused the always. We know what it meant to be sound. What it meant then was that the river was stone. We began thusly: if we were to predict the path or the reaction of the across. If we went back to the water. We were the beneath. Like it was easy. The light came in the same way. Slowly, and it was through the wall. A shot. There in our hands.

Our hunger becomes insatiable. We cannot stop. We finish a sandwich and want soup. We finish the soup and want chicken. We finish the chicken and want cake and frosting and bacon and Swiss cheese and figs and mortadella and haricot verts and peaches and coffee cake and potatoes with gravy and carrots cut into tiny matchsticks and noodles with shrimp and baklava and fried eggs and a salad of watercress and mint and a salad of arugula and apples and a salad of spinach and walnuts and various kinds of pizzas and various kinds of pastries and french fries and toast and lentils and squash and the table will never hold it all, the table will collapse under the weight of all this.

It's as if we made a pact without knowing it. All our shame to pay for. All the ways life makes you ashamed and the way you must pay for it. You can't just turn out the lights. You can't just understand how life works. You can't call the day into being. You can't beat it out of us. We won't know what to tell you. Stop it. Stop it right now. There's nothing wrong with you. Stop it. Stop it and sit down. Sit down or I'll give you something to cry about.

We Will Please

In the empty space between sound and color, we ran reckless through the prospect. Kept still. We walked towards each other with our hands outstretched like sleepwalkers. We pretended to be murdered, our bodies flat on the ground and our arms in angles like police outlines. Mornings, we collected leaves off the lawn. Everything was dying.

We plunged into the hollow. It was already nostalgic, this time of blue and bright and damp hands on the railing.

The portrait of us as girls has faded away. In it, we stand next to each other wearing matching dresses and shoes in front of a fireplace. Our hair is braided into long ropes down our backs. The photographer whistled and cooed like a giant bird and told us to smile, laugh, be happy. It was just before the longest day of the year. We stood in front of the photographer with his camera and held hands, our mouths set in straight lines.

Earlier, we collected eggs from the henhouse, spread feed around the pen, and sang songs. These songs were in a language we didn't understand, but we loved the melodies and had learned the sounds by heart. We took turns carrying the egg basket as we went back up to the house. We stared hard at the sun so we would see spots and feel our retinas wither. We pretended to be blind, our arms outstretched like three miniature Frankensteins.

Breakfast was placed on the table for us: toast with boysenberry jam, soft boiled eggs in pretty cups, slices of fried ham, tea. We sat and quickly ate. We wolfed it down. We said *wolf* and *woof*. We howled like wolves at the table and made our hands into claw shapes. We scratched at the air and felt ancient and wise.

We often felt uneasy. Like a sliver beneath the skin. There but not.

We took the rocks from their holding place and placed them on our chests. The weight of them was comforting. They held us down. As if we would fly off without them holding us there, as if that were possible.

Summers, we would lay ourselves down in the creekbed and pretend we were minnows. We'd walk far into the valley and climb down to the water. It was shallow and clear. As we let the water rush over us, we tried to imagine the end of everything. The water would wash us away to the larger river and into the heavy mud that lingered there. That was as far as we could imagine going. No other movement downstream. Just a short journey that would offer a silence different from the house silence. But of course, nothing is really silent. The creaks of floor boards, the sighing of walls, the rush of water over us, the muffled wind.

Eventually, our hunger would overtake us, and we would emerge soaked, our hair streaming dark down our backs, our dresses clinging to our calves. By the time we walked out of the valley, we were completely dry.

As children, we were more serious than the others. We stared out the window of our bedroom and felt sad. The trees, the flowers, the birds—everything was on its way out. And where did that leave us? Would we be suspended in the window forever?

It was difficult to move away from the pane of glass that separated us from the outside. We tried to play as we saw the other children do. We skipped rope and climbed trees. We slid down slides and ran breathless across the playing field. We picked dandelions and wove them into crowns. We made paintings in art class and walked home from school. It was like we were just like them.

We used to walk the fields with our father to help him gather the growing things. We pulled up weeds and threw them in a big pile on the edge of the field. They sat there in the sun and smelled green and then greener in the heat.

We walked, straggling behind our father in his heavy boots. Smoke from his pipe flew behind him and mixed with the dirt and green smells. The end of summer was a hot mouth on our faces. We were tired and thirsty, but we couldn't say anything. We had work to do.

The field was dry and we had to help it. We carried big watering cans and moved down the rows of corn and beans and tomatoes and zucchini and onions and bell peppers and potatoes and marigolds and lettuce and radishes and cucumbers and carrots. It would be our fault if the field dried up and everything died.

We hoped for rain all morning. We kept looking at the sky, wishing for gray and dark. It was so hot.

Our father said nothing—he just walked and watered and plucked weeds and examined.

All of us were dusty, hot, and tired. We watered the last of the field and began the walk up the hill back to the house. We girls began to run and sing. We were so happy to be finished, so happy to have helped the field.

Our father stayed behind and stood smoking, gazing hard at the sky, hot and blue and cloudless.

Sometimes, when it rained, we would sit on the floor and spread out the maps of the world. We followed the blue lines with our fingers and thought about the journey. We stop at the cities and hold our fingers there. We picture it, the place we've never been, and walk its streets and stand in its doorways. We carry our valises and throw them on the beds of old hotels with bad plumbing and bugs and dirty pink blankets and streaked wavy window glass, and we sit on the windowsills and look out over rooftops and down at the small heads becoming damp with the early evening mist. Everyone is on their way home from work. Here, in the city where we've come to wander, where we do not belong, where we will always be somehow foreign, where the river is different, we find we cannot speak. We sit quietly in our room and mark out the days we spend here with a single black line. Only upon leaving do we realize we want to stay.

This is what the hunger is like.

Persistence is not a virtue. It's pest-like. Annoying. We're an annoyance like a sliver or a constant tap in the wall. Our daydreams shiver in the wind. We have nothing tall to climb. It's underneath everything we know to find out what we do not. How to dig down. To cut through the rock of forgetting. There are glimpses. We've had them. Green glass. Thistles in a vase in a window. Robins in the trees and their noise on the air. An arrangement of fruit in a bowl. We thought it was pretty, the way our mother would arrange the lemons and pears and grapefruits and strawberries and apples and peaches and nectarines and plums and apricots and figs and dates and grapes and cherries and insert sprigs of mint and rosemary and sage and thyme and tarragon and parsley around them all. A forest in a bowl, and we were the giants of the forest looking down upon it. The bowl was a milky green in the morning light. It would take hours, this arrangement. We were forbidden to speak, even to breathe, while she was at work. To put these objects into order meant that everything was in order. When the windows darkened, she took the bowl out and walked it to the street where she dumped it onto the curb without ceremony. She walked back to the house illuminated by the streetlights, the bowl grasped in her hands like a trophy. In the morning, the fruit would be gone or smashed or just as she left it. In the morning, she would begin again. She would begin again each morning, and we would watch her hands placing each piece carefully.

As girls, when the guns were put into our hands, we didn't want to. Holding a shotgun is hard. Heavy and cold and the recoil nearly knocks us over the first time we fire. Say pull and follow it and only shoot when you're sure. Pull and follow and shoot. We became good at it. Really good. We could see for miles. Our timing was impeccable. Our aim was precise. Everyone said we would clean up on the lakes. Ducks and geese. Blinds and boats. Early morning and too cold. Shooting trap was a game. Clay pigeons were not in the shape of flying birds but bright disks. Like someone's idea of a bird who had never seen one.

Only once did we shoot to kill. Just to see. And then when we saw it, limp and heavy, we knew it was over. It was confusing to us that a tiny steel ball could end a life. What did it matter if there was something extra? With glass or clay it made sense: it shattered completely. It was so clear. But a body is different. Sometimes you can't even tell.

Now, the dead are put into our hands and we don't want them. Holding a corpse is hard. Heavy and cold and we recoil from the stench. Say the words and sing and wail and howl and grieve for us, they say. Reach your hands up and don't let them take the coffin out of the house before you're finished. We became good at it. Really good. Everyone requests our presence. Everyone thinks we can help them.

When we were girls, we watched over the fence. We carried buckets. We stayed where we were told to stay. We did as we were told to do. Our one offence was leaving. Our only infraction was taking off that night. We went and said nothing in the face of the faces forbidding us to go.

Woe Are We,
That Our Abode Is Prolonged

The air was thick with smoke. Nothing would penetrate it. When the water came, it felt like glass. We lay there, soaked on the wood floor.

Earlier that day, we ran through the meadow, laughing in the way only young girls can laugh. We knew, although we did not like to think about it, that this phase of life would soon be over.

Our girlhood would be trampled and lost. It would be buried beneath the soft ground where our parents had lain for years now. We pictured our mother, the decay that must have ruined her beautiful face. Our father, only bones.

Half-awake, struggling to sit upright, we looked at each other. Something had changed. We could not define it. Our youth had passed, we knew. But there was something else.

We place our hands over our heads. We wave them back and forth. Our hems hang to the ground and become damp in the wet grass. Every morning it is the same. We must greet the new day thusly. We wave our bodies back and forth like seaweed.

Our bird calls have become more and more authentic. We have practiced a long time in an effort to communicate with the chickadees, phoebes, finches, and flickers. We speak to each other this way, too. The two-tone whistle of the chickadee serves as *where are you* and also *I am here*. The frantic cadenza of the finch can mean many things. We have constructed entire paragraphs of dialogue from the song of the finch.

It is time to go to the river to make our offering. We do this each day. A pebble, a smooth bit of glass, a piece of bright wool. We toss these small objects into the river and concentrate very hard. Then we gather the water in buckets. We march back to town like children with our buckets splashing onto the sidewalk. We are children with buckets of water, we are whistling birds.

One summer, everything kept going up in flames. The sparrows burned in the burning fields. The burning birds tried to fly away but fell blazing to the earth. The stench of burning feathers lasted weeks. There was no water. Everything kept going up in flames.

Inside our chests something was burning. We couldn't identify what it was. We couldn't get it out. As if those sparrows had lodged between our ribs, or a flaming owl sat solid between our lungs. Stuck.

The fire inside us was worse at night when we went around gathering our things. We saved bits of food and kept them on stands next to our beds. A single red cherry in a tiny glass jar. Three perfect peas knocking against each other in a small container. The meat of a walnut wrapped in blue gingham. It was necessary, this hoarding. It was preservation of life, we thought. The most perfect things, the most delicious, must be kept forever.

The flames in our chests made us weary. We were always thirsty, always in the bathtub covered in ice. This fever would not break, yet we knew if the heat ceased we might die. We couldn't remember how long we'd been alive.

What else can we tell you?

The way was difficult and unclear. We walked the path to the river without looking back. Beneath the bridge it was cool and dark. The light came through in specks, and we watched it move on our faces. There in the daytime. We were there in the day and night. We caused the way to falter. It was unclear where the water began. If we were there, it was because we had no choice. If we were there, it was because we knew we couldn't return. Our hands were shaking as if they were not our hands. We didn't know what it meant to be extra, to be always. We didn't know what it meant then. It was hard to predict the reaction of the water to our weight. We sank slowly, and it was just like in a dream: a wall of water followed us. It made a terrible sound. The sound was like a stone we could pick up and throw into the river. We skipped across the water. We were the water then. It was easy. We didn't know it could be so easy. The way down was a straight shot and our hands let go. We let go.

We harbored the fantasy that we could be cured. It involved waking each morning and holding the vision of death in our minds. It involved saying out loud, *We will die. We will die. One day, we too, will die,* to each other, the mirror, and then back at each other. The number three became important. We found ourselves checking the front-door lock three times, saying things in triple, listening to nothing but sad waltzes, drawing flowers with three petals, birds with three wings, arranging objects into triangles. We were reluctant to believe that our beliefs would come to nothing. That what we did was ridiculous, that the various ceremonies we created and followed were nothing but wastes of time. But our luck could not be changed.

What we know:

The weather was horrible

The river was high

It was just before springtime

and the rain froze as it hit the ground

The bridge was icy

but we weren't going that fast

We were just driving

We were dancing when it happened

The radio was on and we were dancing in our seats

A swerve and then into where

we waited a long time

We sank slowly

We plunged into the slowest dance

We waited and stayed until

The future. The future. The future. The future. The future. The future the future the future it comes in waves as if we can see it passing like a barge or girl walking serious down near the tracks leading them all somewhere else, a place unknown to the future. We were so certain once. Once, we were sure. We are not sure now, here in the future. We are not anything but starving. Like the present, the future holds the promise of hunger and the persistence of sorrow. We are sorry for your loss. We are so sorry. We in the wake of it. The waking of it. We wake the corpses by shaking the ropes.

In the past, we spent our days doing nothing. The sweetness of perpetual boredom. It was our only occupation. Mornings were silent except for the crackle of the record player and a long dead voice ringing through the room. A voice alive there, while we sat and listened. Then the voice gone and of course the music was that way too. Into thin air. And the meals. The table heavy with cream and tea and bread and eggs and fruit and juice and the way the jam looked in its jar in the morning light, casting worm-like shadows on the table, like a ruby slowly turning.

We call out and no one can hear us say we're down here, we're stuck, we can't get out, we're lost, we've been waiting so long, we know it's going to be hard to understand, hard to gauge what kind of state we're in, the air seems bad down here and we're starving. All we think of is what we'll eat, and how strange it is to be so thirsty when we're completely surrounded by water.

And now: blood everywhere we look. The ground soaked with it. Like the dead things we'd find off the main road near the creek bed. Flattened and matted and not like anything that was ever alive. How the stain would stay on the asphalt for months, how it would slowly melt into the concrete and then finally disappear. And the sensation of running something over. The dog runs out and it's too late. Stopping anyway and terrible panting and that gaze upward with blood in the eyes and then lying there so still and hot. Thinking, *how stupid, what were you thinking?* Or firing a shot just to do it and then the squirrel limp and horrible. And having to clean it and pulling off the skin was like taking off a little fur coat. Then the stench of it cooking and having to eat it, this rodent, and no one telling us it was a punishment, no one asking, *what were you thinking?*

We emerge shaken every time, as if we thought it would be different. As if this were a place of refuge or solace. But it never happens. And despite this, we will always go back, like pilgrims, like martyrs, like sheep, like ants, like sleepwalkers, like the blind. We will return like the sacrifices we are. The meek shall inherit. The meek shall be exalted. The meek shall be invoked, shall shine, shall fall, shall sink, shall be given up, will give up, will be renounced, will wake slowly to the morning sun streaming in through the window, it was the first light we saw during that summer of storms when we walked through the flood down to the main road, it was nearly impossible to not get carried away, our dresses hiked up and our shoes tied together and slung over our shoulders, we were on our way to town for supplies even though we didn't know whether we could get there, even though there might not be supplies to be had, and we were laughing the whole time, thinking that if this water remained and we had to live in it like we were, that it would put fins on our feet and gills on our faces, and we looked at each other and pursed our lips and made the sounds we thought fish would make if they were like us.

We open the door that reveals the room of our girlhood. The windows are dark and the room dim. We feel its familiar air, its odor of mildew and onions. This room is where we would awake at night with the trees singing in through the windows open to the hot air of late summer. Where we heard the rhythmic, heavy pulse of toads covering the road with their clumsy bodies. It was so loud. Everything in the night of our girlhood was deafening. We could never sleep.

We are searching for something. We are trying to say what we mean. We do not know what to say what to do how to say it how to do anything. We are at a loss. We climb the stairs that look like waves and move toward the doorway that seems close but is actually far away. We feel stupid and awkward and dumb. We forgot how to walk, how to work through a problem. Our ideas have dried up. We are dried up. We are a dry run in the summer heat falling down the hill, falling into the valley in search of a drop of water. Where it flows is mysterious. The mysterious is stupid. The mysterious is lazy. We are lazy. We have nothing to offer. Dried up and spent. We were always so quick with a comeback, with something to say. We were always so clever. All we want to do is sleep.

We go to the river to see. It's dark and light at the same time—the depth of water unclear and awful. We're there to see where we were. It's winter, a light snow coming down over us, leaving a thin film of white on our dark coats. Overhead traffic pounds on the blue bridge lit up in yellow lights. We stand and watch. We stand and look. There is nothing we can learn from standing there. We know we must get in. Where we were was not on the shore.

This is how everything is. We were in the water and then we weren't. No one to bear witness or to mark the time. No one to take a photograph. And how would that happen anyway? You can't take a picture of what you're thinking. You can never do that.

Although we didn't believe it before, we do now: all roads lead into a deep dark ditch. And us, there, just as predicted. Anyone's mother would tell us she told us so.

The curves, the lights, the road slick with rain. The big, white mansion shining like a jewel at the top of the hill.

A dove's nest has been disturbed. The nest hangs out of the tree with the brood inside, frantic and flapping. There is nothing to do about this.

There isn't anything we could have done.

Fail-safe measures line the parking lot. Our personhood has been transformed into something else. It is unclear, at this moment, whether the space we take up is the same. It seems we have wings. In the dream, we had wings.

We walked along the trail deep into the woods. The trees there old, ancient. Walnuts covered our path, green still, and emanating a sharp scent as our feet trampled them into the mud. We were far away from the river, but the creek bed was nearly overflowing.

It's getting harder to remember what it is we are trying to keep close.

There's a diagram that explains the way in which death occurs. It's in the shape of a triangle. We've studied it and see the movement of the arrows that equate marriages with funerals, that point toward return, toward exhumation: a return to the world of the living. There is the world of the living and there is the death world of the living. There is the movement toward the grave and then the retrieval from it. To be wed is to be pointed upward, the point before descent, the world of the death world, the world of the living dead, there is nothing to prevent us from sinking. Sinking isn't like falling, it's like hunger. We long to be gathered together, taken up, we long to be understood as living, we are making our effort to get to the train on time, it's not possible, we've realized this hours ago, yet we pack up our things and look out the window at the weather, trying to predict what the weather will be miles from where we are now. Hurry up, you're going to be late. I'm not waiting. It's your own damned fault if you're late. I'm getting in the car. Jesus Christ, what in the hell are you doing? Come on. Let's go.

A strike out. Complete miss. A gentle gust moves us slightly toward land. We tumbled in and were fished out. Fell in the drink.

And the land seemed made up. We couldn't understand what it meant to stand. The problem with moving further out from shore was growing used to drifting.

If we were left, we were fortunate, although our fortune and our understanding of it wasn't clear at the time. At the time, it was excruciating. We felt hollow and worn. We felt our hearts twisting in our chests. We felt blind, like pigs moving through sticky sludge. Our understanding was limited because everything we knew was veiled. It wasn't real. They told us the blue trees we say we saw appear in our bedroom, or the heavy-winged thing that chattered around our heads late at night, or how the river spoke to us, clearly, in a language we knew, were nothing but lies. But even if we were the only ones to see blue trees and the flying animal flying around our heads and the only ones to hear the river speak, it was enough. We knew we weren't like the others. Always, we knew this. It was the way of the other world, to which we did not belong, and which, no matter how much we studied and observed and tried to learn, we would never really know. Ever. It was removed from us, it seemed. Forbidden. We were in between and would spend our nights weeping, waking with puffy faces, wondering why we had been so isolated, why it was us who couldn't take part, who could learn to be that way, who would never be admitted.

What we were thinking then was that we didn't exist. What we came to know is that we would exist forever.

Our training was grueling. Staying up all hours studying a strange language made from dots and lines. Our hearing was tested, our vision. We were dragged out of bed and asked, *Do you see what is sitting at the window? Do you hear what that person a mile away is saying? No? Why not? Why not?*

The half-moon is bright and we wait. It is harder, now, to tell whether we are physical bodies. When we are all together, it seems so. When we are alone, we feel like a faint vapor trapped in a jar. Unhinged from our limbs.

We sit beneath the big elm in our backyard on a checkered cloth, legs tucked beneath us, wearing light spring dresses. A map is spread out, and we trace the blue roads with our fingers. This kind of travel is quick, and we traverse miles over hills and valleys in mere seconds. Where we go depends on what we want to see, which map we've dragged out of the big green trunk in the front hallway. We are there in the ancient cities, walking near aqueducts, marching over cobblestones. A sparrow lands before us, and we sprinkle breadcrumbs and watch her eat with quick pecks. More birds arrive and we drop more crumbs. Soon there are so many, we cannot see further than our own hands. Soon the birds overtake us and we are covered in feathers and beaks. These birds, with their rapid little hearts, with their tiny darting heads and small glassy eyes, they alight on us and push us down to the ground.

Distant voices fall down the hill above the house where we sit wrapped in blankets. We can hear them but not what they say. It sounds angry, like a mob. Like violins playing together in different keys. Like waiting for nausea to pass while one's head rests on the cool tile floor. The sound is focused and suspended. Frozen like the air outside. Still and cracking.

In between eruptions of yells and cries, we throw teacups at the windows. We tear down the draperies and pull picture frames off the walls. We jump up and down on the furniture and pull the upholstery apart. Feathers and fluff fly around and cover us. A thin fog of dust swirls through the room. This is the only thing we can do. We don't know what else to do.

Our hunger is insatiable. We find ourselves pining for all manner of foods: lamb and carrots and mushrooms and chicken and kale and mustard and ice cream and chocolate and pâté and shrimp puffs and beef stew and rice and beans and escarole and noodles with curry and little crackers with cubes of cheese and various lettuces and other things we have never tasted.

Mostly we eat radishes. Like Rapunzel's mother, we pull the red globes out from other people's gardens. We eat them there, crouched over the green leaves, spitting off the dirt. We move from plot to plot in search of them. We wait until nightfall and creep slowly through the backyards.

We gaze out from our perch on the bluff that rises eastward and overlooks the main channel of the river. It's a bright, cold day. The clouds, puffs of light in the light sky. We are under the assumption it will rain. A storm. The light is greener and things are so still. We'll get caught in it. We'll get caught and will run screeching for shelter and find a meager roof of branches. Our watching will catch the lightning sharp in the sky, and its attendant crash will shake our hearts, shake our feet into the ground. It's dangerous and we know it and we are so glad to be out here. We are so glad this danger is so close and we are watching it. It doesn't even matter what happens. We'll get in trouble, we'll get filthy, covered in mud, and the rain will cover us so completely it will be as if we're inside the river. Our reluctance to leave, to find true shelter, to get into the car: we cannot resist it. Godammit, what are you doing? Why are you just standing there? It's pouring out here! Just come on, get in the car! Now! I'm not waiting. I am not going to wait for you. Fine. Stay here. Just stay where you are. See if I care.

We dream of a boat submerged in a body of water. It's always the same boat: broken masts, the hull torn off. There are women in red dresses, their backs turned, who kneel and look up at the ripped sails, grey and soaring above them like enormous bats quivering in numbers, plunging suddenly and then rising abruptly. Even below water, there's a horizon and a sun that falls and lifts and turns the light yellow and green at the end of the day. Below the ship are dim hills, uniformly triangular and perpetual. On the hills, a brown figure lies prone on the rocks. It's a shadow the boat makes, the broken submerged boat in its disrepair with its kneeling women, making a shadow in the shape of a body on the dim hills of perpetual submersion.

Our kitchen is full of things for cooking: a giant mortar and pestle the size of a small baptismal font, copper kettles, something to remove the cores from apples, a special device to compress the juices from chickens, bones and all, blenders and choppers and openers, herbs on the windowsill, sourdough starter on the counter, pots and steamers, knives for paring, knives for de-boning, knives for slicing vegetables, knives for slicing bread, slotted spoons and colanders, sieves and spring-form pans, china serving platters, silver soup tureens, books and papers with recipes from France and other countries, spices, oils, vinegars, and salts. We have everything we need to make anything we want.

We are unable to think straight. Plagued by headaches, we rest in the dark house. This house where we have stayed for as long as we can remember. Can we remember far back? We have been here a long time. Things are starting to break and wear out. We have to call repair men to fix the broken things after we try to fix them ourselves and fail. We thought some good, strong string would hold the ceiling fan together, but soon enough it broke and the fan came crashing down, breaking a table full of breakfast dishes and nearly slicing our throats open.

In the nimble wind we are shadows. This night is full of dawn and wind and leaves. Our hands are damp, and we look out towards the horizon obscured by fog. We sit on the riverbank with our skirts tucked around our knees, our hands on the rough rocks, our hair in bright scarves. We listen to the flap of silk in the wind, the tiny waves licking the shore. This night is full of fog and we are made invisible by it.

We are here to wait for something to happen. We are here at the river, waiting. We do not know what will appear. We imagine a giant, ancient fish. Or a spectre. A girl in a long gown with long tendrils of hair woven with flowers. The Lady of Shallot.

We do not expect a feeling to pass through us. A sharp sensation, like a papercut, runs the length of our torsos. It is simultaneous and shocking. We don't know what to do. We cry out, *Ah!* and then it is over.

Our fate became clear: We would be at the service of those who leave and those who are left. We had no choice.

We were brought before a tall woman wrapped in a large, black shawl. Her face was old and worn. We kneeled before her and she took our hands in hers and looked deeply into our eyes. No one said a word. After several minutes, she told us to stand and ushered us into a glass atrium where the air was heavy and wet, and flowers like we had never seen were climbing the walls. In the middle of this room of glass, there was a door in the floor. The woman opened the door, revealing a long, wooden staircase. She walked down the stairs, and we followed her. The room we found ourselves in was cool and dark, like a cellar. We were stripped of our dresses by young girls with pale skin who had been waiting patiently for our arrival. The woman poured oil onto our heads. She dragged fistfuls of dirt down our limbs. She led us to a large pit of dirt in the middle of the room and told us to lie there.

We hummed and jostled our bodies. We tried to call out.

Our hearts began to slow, our breath to deepen, and our limbs took on a strange buoyancy. We felt like we were floating. We dreamed of bright green forests, of tables filled with pastries. We dreamed of sun and clouds and water. We mostly dreamed of water.

And Let Perpetual Light Shine Onto Them

Everyone wants to die in their own way. If you ask, you'll get many answers, but most will have this in common: it should be quick, and it should be easy, and it should be painless. There shouldn't be any suffering. I don't want to suffer, they'll say. They say, I would like to die very quickly, unexpectedly. By fire, by ice, by drowning, by accident, by another's hand, by falling, by poison, by rope, by knife, by turning a corner and losing my breath. I'd like to die in a way where the light just slowly dims, but abruptly, without warning. Where I'm in bed surrounded by my loved ones in a white room in a small house by the sea, and no one knows it's the end but everyone's there, just as a coincidence. I'd like to die in a car when I'm seventeen. I'd like to be on a motorcycle or a horse. I'd like to be on my bicycle and suddenly sideswiped. I'd like to be attacked by dogs, by swans, by a gang of thugs. I'd like my lover to do it. I'd like him to hold my hand, stroke my hair, tell me he'll see me soon, and then shoot me in the heart. I'd like to die while eating mint chocolate chip ice cream, while eating a steak, sushi, a plate of fries. I'd like to be struck by lightning, taken up in a tornado, flung out to sea by a hurricane. I'd like to overdose. I'd like to throw myself off a bridge. I'd like to be sitting at my desk by the window at sunrise. I'd like to be dreaming, asleep. I'd like to die in my sleep. I don't care where or when or how, I just know I don't want to be alone.

Living is loud. Breath is loud. Give out the flowers, the stares, the horrified looks that fly across the room. Call the mourners up to the stage. A sad song aches in our teeth. Being sad is easy. It is easier than anything. Inside the cathedrals of our hands, we look through the colored glass. We are made of glass and wood. We are made of glass and wood and water.

There are two variations of weeping.

The dances to fight the war of grief out of the heart are varied and many.

We come to various places.

Our variations linger and spread out across the Western Ghats, the Willamette Valley, Warsaw. We are in Victoria, in Uruguay, in Algiers, in Worcester, in Phoenix. We are on islands, and volcanoes, and the precipice. We stand among live oaks, vegetation. Inside us are swift storms, the season of rain, of tornadoes. The season in which we wear wool, in which we lie down in cools baths. Where we think of all the zebras and yams, of all the wheat and vipers. Where we think of turpentine and typhoons, the definition of valleys, the definition of temperature, the temperate zones and the zone of feathers. We make our attempt.

The funeral towers stand beside the cremation ground. Later they will be torn apart by the crowd. The ashes of the funeral pyre are strewn upon the sea. More than counting and measuring are involved. More than loading and unloading the bones. We carry water. We carry water, rope, and bones.

Too much wailing and no one believes you. Too little and no one believes you. We practice on each other, giving each other notes. We film ourselves and the whole routine: meeting the bereaved and touching their hands with our own, keeping our eyes lowered, making sure our veils are transparent enough for them to see our faces streaming with tears, taking our places in the stiff chairs in our stiff dresses, the songs and the chanting, the howls and wails. We stand in front of mirrors and just cry. We observe other funerals and the wives and daughters and mothers and fathers and sons and husbands who stand stoic by the grave and then suddenly fall to the ground. The sound they make is elemental, like an erupting volcano, or repeated mountains of thunder, or the way a foghorn makes you feel it from inside your guts.

There is nothing exceptional about this. Everyone is attracted to the spectacle. Everyone wants to go to the execution, the funeral, the scene of the crime. Everyone wants to bear witness to that last glimmer. The breath leaving the body, the final gaze outward.

Everyone is so curious. Sometimes they mistake us for their daughters and granddaughters and sisters and wives. We let them believe it. We tell them nothing of our life as girls, our memories of the river and the rain slicked road, our house slowly falling into disrepair, of our insatiable hunger, our dreams of the end that will never arrive, all our impossibilities.

They ask if we just wait around for people to die.

In the dark room, we gather. It's late and the candles show how long everyone has been sitting there. Our garments are gathered around us for warmth, and we shiver with the others. It is unclear how long we are meant to stay here. Our songs have ended, and we've walked hundreds of circles around the table where the corpse lies with her hands folded primly and her face slack and pale.

The other room is filled with bright yellow electric light, and we are led there by a tall man in a dark suit and told to sit in the chairs that line the wall. He leaves the room and comes back with two young girls with plates in their hands. They shove the plates at us. They are full of bitter greens and triangles of bread and butter and deviled eggs and tuna casserole and roast chicken and scalloped potatoes and slices of rare beef and slices of apples and small squares of lemon tart and macaroni salad with mayonnaise and peas and tiny meatballs filled with minced onions and it seems impossible that all this food can fit onto these plates, that these girls are able to carry them, that everything doesn't plummet to the floor, and they give them to us, and we've never held anything as heavy.

Before, there were ropes and rags and a trumpet with which to summon the crowds. Time was kept. Ancient songs accompanied the wails, the rending of flesh, the tearing of hair and fabric. Jangling tambourines offered something solid and ringing. Darkness lifted and hovered over the crowds during the ceremonies and gathered itself into a heavy glowing sphere and entered into us who came and who were paid.

Offerings to the river. Offerings to the air and fire. Then taking the river away, taking away the ashes.

We stand there holding on to what we must offer. It is remarkable we don't stumble. Our strides are steady, but we don't seem to be stepping on solid ground.

We get up and make her do it. Through the streets at dawn walking home, she is alone, and we join her. We sing and whisper, we sing and whistle, we blow softly on her neck, her cheeks, her arms. When she crosses the threshold, we push her to the floor, hold her down, and say, *It's time to go.*

She blinks once in understanding and allows us to move her legs toward the door. Nothing can stop it once it begins. We feel it rise into our throats, burning and horrible, the excruciating hum, it falls out of us.

We take turns circling the body, placing marigolds and rosemary, burning sweet grass, anointing her throat and forehead. We rub salt onto her temples and palms, we brush her hair out of her eyes. We let out a heavy sigh and tell her it's over.

We put on our jackets and get ready to leave. They follow us to the door, carrying dishes covered in plastic wrap for us to take, giving us directions back to the highway, patting our arms, putting on brave faces. *You were good to come. I didn't know what else to do. I wouldn't have been able to do this on my own. I was at a loss. It was hard to know what to do.*

An ancient lament. Burning through the trees. A window full of flames, an orchard. We are calling we are calling we are calling we are calling. We weep for you and you are gone we weep in the trees in the meadow in the leaves in the carpark in the skyway in the architecture in the street. We are standing in the street just standing there we are there in the street and we can't stop crying.

We dream about them.

This woman was always alone. She was waiting for something that never arrived. It was unclear in the dream what it was she was waiting for, but it seems it was probably a lover. A man. Someone she did not know, whom she'd only met once. Perhaps there was a refusal on her part that she regretted and was too shy to reach out after. So she lived in possibility for a while, going places she thought he might be, lingering at a table for hours, nursing a glass of something bitter. Perhaps this man, whom she'd only met once, had forgotten, or disappeared, or moved away, or was run over by a herd of elk. The possibilities of his demise were endless. But she knew the truth, even if she didn't want to admit it: that while there was something about her that was initially appealing, upon further investigating, there was also something about her that was repulsive.

We did not see her weep, but we did see her collect stones and place them into boxes. At night, she took the stones and tied them in a large blanket and placed it on her chest. The weight was comforting. It reminded her she took up space.

One was held down. She couldn't understand what it was that was holding her there. It was difficult to see. The darkness was from inside, it seemed. There were only small sounds.

A chirping bird

Aircraft racing through vapor

The clicking of the blinds against the open window

A drop of water falling into the sink

Muffled conversations on the other side of the wall

Tinny music from the ice cream truck down the street

Her breath in her head

Her heart in her head, her mouth. The beating of it became awful, like a persistent knocking at the door she didn't want to answer.

When did the darkness arrive? It was swift, a flood. The river cresting and covering what was not meant to be covered.

All she could think of was digging in the dirt for potatoes. Long ago. There was a photograph of the piles, the shovels. They stood next to them with their hands over their eyes, squinting into the sun that had been beating down on them all afternoon. Earlier that day, she remembered wanting to be done with this youth, this life of being told. She wanted to sing, to wear extravagant fabrics, line her eyes with black, stain her lips with red. It was no wonder when she came out to the field in her best dress and her cheeks pink from pinching that she was laughed at. Admonished. It was not the time nor the place, she was told. It would never be the time or place. There was a club of women who were foreign to her, the way they seemed all-knowing, the manner in which they moved, how they looked and spoke, and she knew then that she would never be admitted. It was closed to her. Just because she was female did not mean she was like them or would ever be. It was devastating and confusing. How was it that she couldn't know? How was it that the information she needed and sought was out of her reach?

And at the end of her days, she lay pinned. Held down by nothing she could see. And it was over finally. It was finally done.

One was lost in the grid of the city in which she had lived. Each road kept leading to the same spot: a small storefront where they sold strange things like pigs' ears and smoked carp. The walls were covered in cheap, dark paneling. We wandered the aisles and picked up objects and put them back down. It seems we were sent to buy something, but we were unclear what it was. We knew we would know when we saw it. We searched for what seemed like days. Wandering through the tiny shop, we saw her wandering too. She was alternately a young woman and an old woman, and sometimes she was an old woman with a young face and sometimes a young woman with an old face.

Another stood waiting for the bus. She stood there in a small patch of sun. It was cold, winter. We stood with her and watched as she tore paper into strips and let them fall to the ground, into the puddles the sidewalk was covered with. The paper was full of writing we couldn't read. The ink blurred and smeared together when it landed in the water.

One sat in a straight wooden chair and stared out the window, his hands on his knees. His face was blank. As in, he had no face, no features. His face wasn't there in any way that was recognizable. Yet we knew he was smiling. He was laughing so hard he was crying.

Another had stayed in her house for days at a time. She couldn't bring herself to leave the comfort of the windows and walls that enclosed her. It was like this until the very end. We could see her indoor face on her face when we came. We knew her eyes, although closed now, had not seen a far-off vista in months, that the light had not penetrated her skin. She was bone pale, and it was as if her limbs were softer than other limbs.

Her son explained this to us. He said he tried to coax her away, tried to make her take even just one step over the threshold, but she refused. When he asked why, she only said it was impossible. It wasn't something she could do. The world was no longer hers, it was no longer for her, so, she said, she must stay in the world she had made, the one that was hers, that was for her, and the other world, the one outside, could have everyone else, everyone else could have it.

Besides, she said, I can look out the window when I am lonesome for what I used to know.

The son, in honor of this, had moved into her apartment so that he could keep her ashes there in her own world.

We stayed until just past nightfall, calling and wailing and making our steps around her body. We didn't have the heart to tell him she had finally left and, despite the ashes he would place tomorrow in a ceramic urn on the fireplace, she wouldn't be coming back.

All of the skeletons beneath the earth. All of the daffodils ready to bloom. All of the trees in their autumn decay. All of the gardens drooped over their fences. All that's buried in the riverbeds. All those who turn from their reflections. All the rain that falls. All the small things that hide in corners. All that contains joy and goodness. All of the stones. All of the light. All of the living and all of the dead.

Another family, another landscape, another act of contrition. The flickers will yell and fly overhead. The cars will age as they drive down the highway, as if the past were dust, as if the past could become solid, a silent visitor who presses into the chest. We hold our palms over our hearts in order to keep the vibration closer, in order to say *we are so sorry for your loss.*

Arriving early, we walk the grounds. A fallow field. A split-rail fence. The sky big and heavy. A woman stands near a small herb garden going to seed. She stands very still, her hands to her sides, her pale-pink coat flapping in the wind against her calves, her pocketbook under her arm. She stands and a heavy fog floats low. Slowly, it begins to make a circle around her and splits her body in two. Her head becomes severed. It hovers. It begins to drift away from her, and everything turns dark as it moves.

It is nearly dawn by the time we finish, and we are exhausted and thirsty. We drink buckets of water. We splash water on our faces from big white bowls the family servant brings to us. We are brought to the long table and are asked to sit, to eat. We sit and cannot believe the amount of food. Tureens full of shrimp bisque and lobster bisque and clam chowder, cherry tarts and tarts of leeks, a leg of lamb, a pile of chops, a beef roast surrounded by potatoes and onions, a sea bass on a platter, its eye cloudy and its tail curled, cassoulet, sausages and salamis, Roquefort and Swiss and Camembert and gouda, and a tower of chocolate, and a tower of macaroons, and a cake with the departed's name writ upon it, a dish full of raspberries, another of mints, bread and butter, and hundreds of deviled eggs.

We are told to eat it all.

They make patterns in us. If viewed from above, we look like something resembling a riverbed, a pathway where currents cut across themselves and where the water and land merges. We dip our fingers into the font and walk into the church.

By this Holy water and by your Precious Blood, wash away all my sins, O Lord

We join the ranks of those who have left. A true and proper mirror of lack. But we remain. We feel we are always en route to the end of the line, but we never seem to arrive. The ocean could swallow us there. If we could get to the gulf, that open mouth, it could take us in and swallow us whole. We could rest then. It would finally be quiet.

Onward to the fallow fields. Marching in step, a dance of sorts, we gather the fields, we take them up in our hands, all the wheat and willow, the sparrow and minnow, there is a storm on the horizon, and we know this storm. It is every storm we've ever encountered. This storm, it lives in us, we have it inside, there is nothing to be done once it's released—there is nothing we can do once it happens. We brace ourselves in the middle of the street, in stores, in restaurants, in the houses where we gather to pull at our hair and scratch our faces and wail until it's time to stop.

We are driven to the country. Dark. The roads become narrower as we move deeper into the valley. As if we will actually reach the vanishing point. We get out of the car and hear nothing but birds. All kinds of calls and chirps and whistles. A house in the middle of nowhere. Our coats are taken from us at the door by a short, grey woman, and we are led into the bright aviary at the back. The birds flit around us, land, and take off again, looking at us expectantly. We are overcome with the urge to teach them to speak. It's as if it's why we came. We focus our attention on a medium-sized grey one with a long, black beak. We circle around him and say, *Hi*! We say it again and again, our voices high-pitched and overly friendly, and we think this will encourage him. We say it again, *Hi!!!* and the bird opens its beak and makes a noise that sounds nothing like the word. Again, we persist, and finally, the bird says it, *Hi!* and flies through the door we left open.

In the chapels. In the cathedrals. In the small country churches. In the basements of churches. In their rooms in the dark. In their kitchens. In their doorways and hallways. Inside our heads. In our minds, they spoke. They spoke through us. We do not know how to explain this. It was not like voices. It was not like thought. It was both inside and outside. A different language. When we spoke for them, we had curious voices. When they spoke through us, we were not ourselves. And it was hard to remember. We couldn't remember afterwards what we said.

It didn't always happen. It wasn't always the case that they would choose to do this. We could never predict it. And we had our own words, our own voices, and we knew the order, the rhythm, the songs. All of the songs we sang, we did this without thinking. We sang and sent them out—as if on a boat, as if on a train, a final farewell, our arms raised over our heads. We waved our bodies back and forth, the motion moving them out. We had to move them out.

And the incense and the smoke and the journey to these places, walking in single file, walking slow, to the gravesides, to the mausoleums, to the pyres piled high, and the tossing of dirt, the setting of fires, ash and wind and water, the water takes everything away.

And she was of the water and the earth. And he was of the water and the earth. From the earth we arise, to the earth we descend. Back from whence we came. A crossing over. To begin again. To begin is to end is to begin again.

When we go to the families of those who leave, we must look them in the eye and agree that it was all for the best, that they never suffered, that life must go on as usual, that certainly he or she was cheerful right up to the very end, that he or she had no idea it was his or her time of departure, that he or she had nothing but happiness in his or her heart, that everything was and will continue to be fine.

It relieves them of the duty of feeling. They don't want to catch the disease of mourning, of grief. It's easier to feel they are doing what they should be doing, paying for the plot, the coffin or cremation, inviting everyone, preparing the food. As if it were a party. As if it were just any other celebration.

Death is invisible. Now you see them, now you don't. Out of sight, out of mind. Disappeared. Spirited away. Up in a puff of smoke. Poof. But this isn't how it happens. This is always just one part of the lie. We tell it over and over. We reassure, we wail, and then we, too, leave.

It's hard to comprehend what people say to us in broad daylight. Only in dark rooms can we actually understand. One morning, the sun came in through the curtains and burned a hole in our foreheads. The daughter spoke to us. We stood dumbly staring at her. It was difficult. We saw spots and nearly fainted. She took us into the front room and gave us glasses of water and then sat us down on the sofa. For a moment, we forgot why we were in this bright room with this stranger. It was humiliating. We felt judged. We looked at ourselves in the heavy mirror across from us. The daughter of the dead woman flirted with us as if we were there to admire her mystery. We were not there to admire her mystery. We were there to mourn her dead mother, dead for a week. We were there to do the job she should know how to do herself. When we finally recovered from our light-induced stupor, the sun had set. We had been staring at her and at ourselves in the mirror since noon. It was hard not to stop breathing. We got up and went to the bedroom where the dead woman lay. We took our places and began our lamentations. We were loud and dramatic. We outdid ourselves. We tried to make our own mystery, to make the daughter of the dead woman jealous of us. But we knew we were the last thing she wanted to be. She would never want to do what we do, look like we look, exist like we exist. We believed for a while—while we were wailing—that she was jealous, and we took great pleasure in this. But by the time we left and she closed the door to her dead mother's apartment, we realized how stupid we'd been.

We are sentenced to speechlessness once the ashes are strewn. The wind blows fiercely and makes the fabric of our dresses audible. Our eyes water.

As we walk back to the car, we begin the dance that will shake our speech back into us. With our arms above our heads, we begin a slow quaver that moves down our bodies. When it reaches our feet, we become frantic, as if covered in ants or mice. We jump and pound our feet quickly up and down. Something like electric shocks course through us and we start wailing again. This is the final stage. The noise is considerable. We fall. We are covered in mud, blinded. We claw at the ground, trying to regain calm, trying to be quiet.

We say *river* and mean *flood*.

We say *comfort* and mean *loss*.

We prepare a bundle for her to take on her journey. It's full of things she might need after: *water, wine, thistles in the jug*. We build a house for her future, and then we tell her to go away.

We construct a web of string and tie ourselves together. We sit for three days.

In the graveyards, motion is scattered, and it's hard to tell what is shadow.

Everything glides toward assembly and hunger.

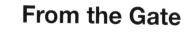

From the Gate

Our problem, our task with the dead, with those who are left, moves into something else. We are dried up, crawling on small, wooden feet. We try to find the way as we did before, by moving to say what we mean, by moving slowly. We have been sinking to the bottom for a long time now. We are going to tell you how this is, what it feels like. Here's this story: it was quick and swift, and we didn't realize how deep the water was at first. We were at a loss to grasp at the straws. We were too lazy to get up. What happened was this: we became old and stupid, and we won't tell you our dreams anymore. We aren't going to claim we are of the water, the mud, the bottom of the river. We aren't going to tell you how we do it—how we abandoned ship, how we were all dressed up with nowhere to go, how we were all bent out of shape, our hands stranded on the shore, how we were all ears, how it was all in a day's work, how all's well that ends well, how we were all over the map, that we were always bridesmaids and never the bride, and we were armed to the teeth and asleep at the wheel. How bats were in our belfries, that we beat a dead horse. That we were beggars, not choosers and never the belles of the ball. How we bent over backwards and got kicked in the teeth. That we bit the bullet, we bit the dust, we flocked together in our gilded cage, and that we would never build a better mousetrap. That we were chewing nails and spitting tacks. How it was a clean sweep, our tumbling into the drink, come hell or high water, they said, cool your jets, they said, but we couldn't fight our way out of a paper sack, we couldn't tempt fate like that, and we bit the hand that fed us, we counted all of the chickens, we rocked the boat, we shot the messenger and dropped like flies, and they said it was even Steven, that the dog's day in the dark cloud's silver lining was an eye for an eye, but nothing comes out in the wash when you've got mouths full of mud, when falling head over heels is a far cry from having a feather in your cap. We had to get out of Dodge, get our ducks in a row. We had to give an inch, our right arm. We had to give everything away when we were out on a limb. We grinned and bore it with our hats in our hands. It was hard to swallow, being hung out to dry, and it was then we found the hate in our guts, the learning of lessons, the eating of crow, not having the last laugh. We were highway robbers then, hitting the books, the bricks, the road, the sack. We held every phone and horse. We were waiting for our place in the sun. In one fell swoop, we were dragged out in the nick of time, then put in the hot seat. We'll make this long story short: the problem with the river is no ladders.

In the Age of Beautiful Death, the departed hover above the river. They lie in the air horizontally and make a straight line with their bodies, one after the other. We follow the procession with our eyes. We wish them well, standing there with our hands on our heads, looking out over the water.

In the Age of Silent Death, they inhabit walls and windows. They chatter and chirp like bats and wait for nightfall. When they leave the roost, they plummet without grace into the open air and wobble through the night on leathery wings. They open their mouths and take everything in.

In the Age of Tame Death, there is nothing to notice. A grey cloud. A shadow on the floor. An unexpected gale. A quick night. We lean with one arm against the truck while the stranger changes the tire. His coat flaps in the wind, and we try to stay out of the way. We try to be encouraging. It's hard to see in the dusk. It's colder than it's been for some time, and we pull our thin sweaters tightly around our bodies.

In the Age of Living Death, we are all standing together.

Clouds hover low, and we walk beneath them, trying to feel heroic. We should be wearing capes or crowns. We should be holy or royal.

Instead, we are unseen, unremarkable, unwanted, and alone. We try to imagine ourselves in a parade, all the spectators leaning into the street, impatient for a glimpse of us, the ones who are coming through their town just for a moment, just for the hour it takes to get down Main Street. They hope to touch the hems of our garments, to take a photograph. They hope we will be kind.

We were kind. We smiled graciously at strangers. We waited patiently for the old man to count out his change to the cashier. We watch a man watch his beloved get on the bus, smiling sadly, holding a hand to his heart, walking toward her just a few steps, knowing he cannot follow, and see him lift his arm and wave for as long as he can see the bus, longer than he could possibly see her in the window where she looks back and waves too, and we weep for them both, the sadness they must surely feel and how it will be for each of them to go to their separate rooms, alone at night, arriving in the dark, and the night sounds of the city buildings in which they live will startle them both, and they will go to bed feeling hollow and wake in the middle of the night because they have forgotten where they are exactly and they thought the other person was there, they really could feel breathing, the weight of another body, but it is not true, it's a dream, and they sit staring into the dark for a few minutes and then go back to sleep, hoping to dream this same dream and hoping it will feel real, and that they will be happy, that the day and its bright light will come slowly, and they can linger in this dream together for a few hours and forget.

There are no others like us, we at the end of night, our starry heads lingering embers on the hearth, our darkness looking out across the river. This life to which we will grow accustomed. This worship of the buried. Groundswells. Estuaries. The waves.

Most days we feel like nightmares passing through unfamiliar towns and apartments and streets and houses and yards and highways. The more we try to be cheerful (we talk about our dog for example), the darker we become. We can see it in their eyes—the fright—and then the slow, backward steps away.

As if they know. As if they can taste it. As if we have a large red letter L on our chests. L for Liar. They think, *here come the liars, come to make their lies, they lie down beside the corpse and lie through their teeth.* We draw our hoods over our heads as we leave and lean into the wind.

We are the only ones who can help them, but sometimes our voices are not enough.

The departed's family and friends look to us to give them absolution. But we do not have the power of providing them with penance. We cannot bestow benedictions. We cannot witch away anything. All we can do is place marigolds around the body, anoint it with oils, conjure the ancient Greek. We can step around the casket with quick taps of our hard, black shoes, bang our tambourines and wail until it looks like we're weeping. We can do all of this, but we cannot change what happened.

All of them say they do not know what to do. They repeat it: I just don't know what to do. What am I supposed to do now? I have no idea what to do. You were good to come. I didn't know what else to do. I wouldn't have been able to do this on my own. I was at a loss. It was hard to know what to do.

We say: *The river always returns to its home.*

We tell them: *There was nothing else you could have done.*

We try to make the current moments become distances.

In the line of fire there is the silence of breath. A heart turning into a branch of a dying tree. The absence of bloom and the resentment embedded in the barren buds. Sit quiet in the blue room and look out the window. Sip something sweet while the storm attacks. Gather up the road in fistfuls. Another opening. Sit until something comes. We may very well sit forever. Nothing can take up the time it takes to wait.

We have learned that nothing anyone can tell you can really prepare you for how you will feel when it happens. There is just no way to know how much you will miss someone, for example, and for how long. No one says you will feel this way forever, but you will. The idea that "time heals all wounds" is a horrible lie. Time is like lemon, like salt in the wound. A grain of sand, a pebble in your shoe. It will never go away and there is no way to explain what that will feel like. There is no way to prepare and you will be reminded of the person at all hours. Every minute holds the possibility of sorrow. Every second. It will arrive when you least expect it. You cannot foresee. There is no prophecy that will give you an indication. There is nothing that will help you.

We walk hand in hand. We run. We're in a neighborhood we shouldn't be in. It's dark and shadowy, and the heavy concrete buildings make heavy concrete angles.

There are others. They stand and watch us. They mill about. They look like they know we've taken a wrong turn, that we've found ourselves in trouble

We wanted this trouble. We decided it.

And then, after running so fast we felt our chests vibrating, our lungs too weak to take in air, we stopped. We turned. We walked calmly back from where we came.

It was then the wall of water came. It howled like a siren. We felt its fingers on our necks. We couldn't look back but we knew what was coming.

They are preoccupied with their losses. They do not hear us. We try to understand. We try to be generous. We try to not let it bother us. We try to focus on other things. We try to be generous. We try to speak up. We try to be louder. We are reluctant to say: *Listen.* We are hard-pressed to call out: *Stop. I'm telling you something.* We try to be generous. We cannot bring ourselves to pound our fists on the table, we cannot storm out of the restaurant without our jackets, without paying, leaving things behind, walking in the rain towards the station and getting onto the first train that arrives down there where things are greenly dark and sitting on the green seat staring at our own reflections, watching them flit and stray across the glass, watching them appear and disappear. We think we have no idea where we're going, that we'll get off at the next stop, but we don't. We stay on to the end of the line and then turn around and go back. We stay on that train all night, in the clanging and clattering, and wonder at our capacity to take things in, at our ability to listen, and how we used to think everyone was like us, that everyone was the same, but it's not true and there is nothing to be done. No one will change. We think about the departure a lot, but it seems impossible. It is impossible. We are slowly losing our way of speaking, our sense of speech, our understanding of language. We cannot understand what we used to understand. We are losing.

We are not patient. We have no flowerbeds to tend, no herbs to cultivate. It is hours before sleep and we are pacing the floorboards. We are not patient. It is understandable to dislike the day, to fall through the various hours of light. We ignore the light coming in green through the window. We sit on our hands and wait rather than prick needles into cloth, rather than write lists onto scraps of brown paper. It is our lack of patience that drives us to distraction and boredom. We have been waiting so long. We wait but do not know why. Yet, we do know something: our daily passage to the river. We know we must go each day. The river with its current traveling muddy and south, bound to lose what it attracted earlier upstream, we understand its significance. We sit on driftwood and ponder the idea of lack, of loss, of early morning refuge. We cannot be more specific, we think. We try, and our words come out half formed. A formal expanse to cross, we think. Winters, it is no better. The ice is a more visible reminder of what is left behind. It is our duty to understand and find out. It is our duty passed to us by no one we have met. In outbursts of anger we have no remorse. In gales of laughter we are vivid and bright. All the many lies we profess as truth to each neighbor's inquiry is offered with only grace, only calm. Our storm lies within and we have nothing to temper the gales. Cloudbursts and hurricanes soak us inside. Our organs damp and floating. Our queries damp and floating. They have not been addressed. We have been waiting longer than anyone. We are at the end of our patience.

We decide to stop.

It's too much. We wave our hands in front of our faces in an effort to halt the tears of frustration that spill down our cheeks, as if to wave away our faces entirely. It's too much to bear. We say this out loud. We cannot take on everyone. We cannot think about everyone. We are only three. We are only small, and we are not holy. We cannot provide what is necessary. Our time here should be over. We should be floating to our end, our demise, we should be exuding sparks or dust or something other than this life we keep moving through.

And the wind howls in our heads, our heads full of fire, we need something cool to drink, anything, a bucket of dirty water, a barrel of ice chipped off the highway. Years ago, when the flood waters rushed across the road, there was no way out. We were so far away from everything except the water. Just us and our frenzy and the rushing rivulets. What happens now? We worried about running out of supplies. When we calculated our rations for each day, it was comforting. Just knowing exactly how long everything would last, to see if there were other ways to extend a meal. And then everything covered in mold, spoiling. We didn't account for that. What happens when everything's gone bad? Just eat it. Better than a kick in the teeth. Better than nothing. And nights by the fire, keeping it lit to save matches. And then, after several days, we woke to the sun blazing through our windows so dazzling we could barely see, could barely think. We didn't understand it. We thought we would always be in this dream. It was the last time we thought we could die.

Last night the dark came early. It crept into our hands and we held it. We shoved it into our mouths and swallowed. The dark was inside us and we could barely see. We sat on the fire escape staring at the back alley where every night the revelers come. They all come through this way. They wear costumes or unremarkable things. They are quiet—just their steps clacking on the pavement—or they yell. There are cats and pigeons, and probably rats, but we can't see anything with the dark inside us. As the hours pass into nighttime, the light does not fade. It stays bright and light and no one seems to notice.

We think we hear strangers in the house. It's early, the light barely visible on the horizon, and there are noises downstairs—bottles being knocked over, the scrape of furniture being pushed across the floor, a heavy cough, voices mumbling low.

We grasp our cotton wrappers close to our necks and sit at the edges of our beds. We look toward the door and then back at each other. After several minutes of listening so closely and so intently we cannot tell whether the sounds are real anymore, we know what we must do. Slowly and with great care, we descend the stairs.

The creaking floorboards give us away. We stop and balance against the banister. We wait.

Silence. The heavy, close feeling of breath stuck in the lungs. The morning birds begin to sing, and the light grows bright and clear.

If the strangers are there, if they are there to kill us, we are ready.

Nothing but shapes of grey where it once was bright and clear, and we were unknown then. There were no expectations then. Then, we were leaving. We left by night and weather. We swerved into what we thought we wanted to be. And then left there. The night full of insects and noise. We were warned and we didn't listen. They came out to try to persuade us to stay, to at least wait until the storm stopped. But we were dead set, and we got into the car, and we turned on the radio, and it was a song we could sing along to—it was like breathing—the steam rising on the windows, the storm wild around us, we drove through it.

A bird has hatched from its egg and now sits downy and bewildered on the window ledge. The effort to fly is borne into its wings. There are no letters to describe this. No letter will be written to describe this moment. A photograph, taken as the young bird leaps to its first flight will be blurred. It will be unclear.

In the morning, there's a crash. Something clangs through the neighborhood. Metal shoved into concrete. All the houses are being torn down and no one knows what they're doing.

We sit and wait. We sit and wait for the noise to cease. The frenetic buzzing, the barely audible crackle of electricity through wires, the pale wind summoned by moth wing, by lace wing. This is our position. We three sitting in a line in dark dresses. We sit in hard wooden chairs to wait. We have been told. We obey.

The red moon waits outside the door. A quick wind chatters the window frames. We sit on the floor and write in small, black notebooks. We take pictures of each other and tuck them between the pages. We will not return to the black hole of our past. We will not do it.

A congress of field mice follow each other through the damp grass in a long brown line. We can hear their tiny feet, their small breath. We see them in our heads, we don't even have to look. We never have to look.

Coursing through. The bottom reveals itself as solid. We measure the distance with a finger held up above our heads. We worry this time it won't happen. We soar and dip. We plummet. Water is air is fire is earth is water is air is nothing.

No one to bear witness. Not before or during or after. As if it never happened. This never happens: up in a puff of smoke. Poof. Now you see me.

Long ago:

The water rushing and the mud slippery and the wheels losing their grip, an angled turn, axle stuck, and then

And now:

Heavy air and the weight of objects. The clutter and the wildness. The country is only the country. Time and our resignation.

This is the persistence:

The private death of someone lying in bed. Someone crossing a street, a body of water. The daily dying everyone else is a part of. Like everyone we've ever known.

We wake and are followed into the street by the chrysanthemums covered in ice, the umbrella of cold fog over the city in which we were placed.

The rains came too late and everything was slick and dark and shiny. We had to slide down the sidewalks, clutching each other's elbows. We all went down in a pile, howling and clutching. We had to crawl home like animals.

In the houses, the ones we peered into at dusk as we made our way home, we watched them carving chickens and roasts, peeling potatoes and carrots, blending gravy and drinks, frosting cakes, baking pies. We watched them watch each other walk from room to room, making footprints in the carpet, making faces in the mirrors. Some simply sit in a chair in a corner, others make gestures, their mouths making word shapes. We heard nothing but our own movement along the pavement and ice. We thought of the conversations they might be having but never thought to have our own.

If they saw us, what would they see? How could they understand the distance between them and us and the rapid night?

Like a hole that can't be filled. It overtakes all thought, all action. This appetite, this internal famine, this constant starvation. We're greedy in our cravings. Always a handful of something in our pockets, always shoving something into our mouths. Nothing will appease it. Like throwing money down a rat hole. Like a whirlpool or quicksand. We can't take in enough. There isn't enough.

Our chests feel as though they will constrict so tightly that we'll suffocate, and the fear of this fear, it just perpetuates it, makes it stronger. Like ourselves, it is ravenous. Always clamoring to be fed. As if it were a pet. A dog or hamster or cat or fish. A bird pecking away at a pile of seeds.

Entering the tomb: hook, line, and sinker. Should it fail. Should the journey be thwarted. Should we forget the melody, the songs. Should we forget anything. The final details are the most difficult to complete.

The phase of negated death appears on the horizon. It appears like a dove on the sill, cooing. Like a sky filled with rain clouds, a plane with a message flying behind on a string. We stare at it in an effort to read the message and hear sawing violins, cymbals crashing, piano notes falling slowly down the staircase.

It's late and we're running. We're running and we feel ridiculous, as if our legs forgot how. We wobble and dart along. We wave down the cab.

On the highway. Entering the town. Fish, hook, and line. Should it falter. Should our arrival be received without ire. Should our lateness be forgiven.

To forgive is a definition of wind. We stood there on the precipice and pulled our sweaters close while the wind whipped our hair into tangles. It was horrible, standing there waiting for an answer. We knew the answer. We already knew it.

It is our way to know and not know. Just like everyone else. There's nothing to tell, ever. We can recount our pasts, but we don't really remember. There was a place, a house, and we lived there. The air was heavy. It was like being underwater. And there was a river and we were racing somewhere and then we were in it. Somehow. We think so.

Or, we were taken away. We were left underground, and then someone came to pull us up by our wrists. Our wrists were dirty and the hands that grasped us felt hard and gritty and we had to rub our skin after, to remove that feeling.

The place was a place that took you into itself and held on. It wouldn't let you go. It would never let you out of its sight. It enclosed you like a chrysalis or tomb.

If we had known, we still would have done whatever it was that we did. It was impossible to breathe among all those leaves, the canopy of trees and insects and a heavy sky—it was like a bag of rocks on our chests. We couldn't breathe.

We cannot stop. We sit and cry and we cannot stop it. If we were ancient, if we were settlers, if the desert came to greet us, if we stand at the doorway alone in our robes, if we rode the horse on the rim of the vase, we could contain ourselves there. If later, the inscription read, *and there they lie, quiet,* if we were less sensitive to light, we who come from the earth, unburied, exhumed, we of the finch, of the sparrow and vine, we who sing, who come to repay our debts, we are not stopping, we continue, we go on, we are under the sign of changes, we will never stop.

How many ways to tell you. The car moved snake-like across the road. It was like it had wings. Something extra. There were sheets of rain, then sheets of water like a crisp sheet pulled from the clothesline and thrown over the bed. Hot. It was so hot and humid. An oven. The storm on its way, then the storm overhead.

Before, we sat in the shade pulling ice cubes down our foreheads, slumped in lawn chairs. Magpies jumped around in the tall grass and we looked up through the branches that cast bright shadows on our faces. We called out to the birds to come to us, come here, come over here, our hands outstretched and pretending to hold a seed, a bread crumb. The day was departing, and we were disappearing into the dusk. Come in, it's time to come in now, come on, it's late, and we get up slowly, our hands dripping, moving as if in a dream, we crawl up the hill.

Notes

The section titles are adapted from "The Office for the Dead at Vespers," a prayer cycle found in the Canonical Hours of the Catholic, Anglican, and Lutheran churches, and recited for the rest of a departed soul.

The "dream of a boat submerged" takes Giovanni di Paolo's painting, "The Miracle of Saint Nicolas of Tolentino" as its inspiration.

"all of the living and all of the dead," references the last line of James Joyce's story, "The Dead."

"By this Holy Water and by your Precious Blood, wash away all my sins, O Lord" is a quote from the Catholic prayer to be recited when using holy water.

"water, wine, thistles in the jug" is quoted from Barbara Guest's poem, "Tessera," from the collection *Fair Realism.*

The sentence, "We try to make the current moments become distances," is adapted from the title of an essay on Helen Frankenthaler's paintings by Barbara Guest, "The Moment becomes the Distance," and discussed in a conversation with Susan Howe on her Poetry Program on WBAI-Pacifica Radio, April 13, 1978.

"fish, hook, and line," is quoted from PJ Harvey's song, "Hook," from the album, *Rid of Me*.

This book is a work of fiction and wholly derived from my imagination. However, I did consult the following texts which helped me shape certain aspects of the characters as well as my thinking about the rituals of mourning: Phillipe Aries' *The Hour of Our Death: The Classic History of Western Attitudes Toward Death over the Last One Thousand Years* (translated by Helen Weaver); Roland Barthes' *Mourning Diary* (translated by Richard Howard); Peter Metcalf & Richard Huntington's *Celebrations of Death: The Anthropology of Mortuary Ritual;* and *Death, Mourning, and Burial: A Cross-Cultural Reader*, edited by Antonius C.G.M. Robben.

This book is also indebted in various and indirect ways to the music of Amália Rodrigues, Lorine Niedecker's poems, the third movement of Brahms' third symphony, Tarjei Vesaas' *The Ice Palace*, and Virginia Woolf's *The Waves*.

Acknowledgments

Thank you to everyone at Noemi, especially Emily Kiernan.

Thank you to the editors of the following journals who published excerpts from this novel (sometimes in radically different versions): *Bombay Gin, Peacock Online Review, Trickhouse,* and *Caketrain.*

Thank you to the editors of New Herring Press, especially Jason Schwartz, for publishing an excerpt of this novel as a chapbook.

Thank you to Lesley Yalen for recommending Tarjei Vesaas' *The Ice Palace.*

For their invaluable suggestions, unwavering support, and continued friendship, I am eternally grateful to Laura Davenport and Selah Saterstrom (with special thanks to Laura for her always-remarkable insights).

To Little Elvis and Griffith Morgan—thank you for being with me.